Zafia Writer

Happy
Tears

New Delhi • London

BLUEROSE PUBLISHERS
India | U.K.

Copyright © Zafia Writer 2024

All rights reserved by author. No part of this publication may be reproduced, stored in a retrieval system or transmitted in any form or by any means, electronic, mechanical, photocopying, recording or otherwise, without the prior permission of the author. Although every precaution has been taken to verify the accuracy of the information contained herein, the publisher assumes no responsibility for any errors or omissions. No liability is assumed for damages that may result from the use of information contained within.

BlueRose Publishers takes no responsibility for any damages, losses, or liabilities that may arise from the use or misuse of the information, products, or services provided in this publication.

For permissions requests or inquiries regarding this publication, please contact:

BLUEROSE PUBLISHERS
www.BlueRoseONE.com
info@bluerosepublishers.com
+91 8882 898 898
+4407342408967

ISBN: 978-93-5989-030-2

Cover design: Shivam
Typesetting: Namrata Saini

First Edition: October 2024

Acknowledgements

I would like to thank my

Late maternal great-granduncle Behram for settling on the balcony opposite mine.

Late maternal grandparents Shirin and Kavas for making my holidays special.

Late paternal grandparents Khorshed and Cawas for watching a movie or two with me.

Late maternal aunt Veera for always attending to me and pampering me every time I vacationed at Bombay.

Mummy Khorshed and Papa Kaikhusroo for large birthday cakes.

Teachers in school and teachers outside for their politeness and their nurturing.

Friends who are there for me *and*

Well-wishers and supporters who are always wondering what I am up to!

"To,

The little, young and old,

Happy Reading!"

Hi _____, I'm Heather Barter,

Wondering with each passing day why I'm not growing taller.

I live with my mum and dad in the City of Pearls,

I am seven, skinny, and have brown skin with thick black curls.

Residing with me is my cousin Omi Wash,

Who hurt his left pinkie the day before playing squash.

On Saturday mornings I sit at the breakfast table eating a big piece of cheddar,

Waiting eagerly for my chocolate milkshake and cheese sandwiches with butter,

Only this time I am trying to read cousin Omi's college acceptance letter.

He hails from Mysore and is currently on a holiday,

Two months from moving far away.

Architecture is what my chubby cousin chose,

'I am elated!' he said, eating tofu and blowing his not-so-long nose.

I wonder how he'll build homes,

He sketches me colourful domes.

'Oh Boy! Really?' I ask excited,

'Yes, four years from now,' he replies delighted.

Browsing Google he shows me vibrant models and spaces,

Looking at houses and buildings I gleefully shout, 'You're going to build fancy doodles. Have fun cousin, toddles!'

Ma'am Jinky Whiskers in complexion and by nature is fair,

She mostly dresses in fabric minky and owns a shelter home for pets,

Encouraging families to adopt hamsters, dogs and cats,

To live with these lovelies and their adorable mess.

I am in class 2,

The desks and chairs are arranged like an Igloo.

We are discussing about the Intra Annual Craft Competition for Juniors,

Ma'am Jinky and the rest ask the five most shy to suggest,

Popeye, Ninja, skyscraper, hot air balloon and castle,

We make the list of materials and stationery,

And fill the big beige ceramic clay, purple paw-printed pot with all that is necessary.

Meet my mummy Jaya and my daddy Ajay,

In Kolkata they met and soon got set.

Journeying in trains is what my lean and sable-skinned mummy likes,

My chubby and light-skinned daddy prefers flying and loves riding bikes.

A week-long trip to the mountains,

Relaxing in nature and visiting a monastery,

Earned the couple a much needed peace-a-plenty.

In her attire and behaviour she is plain,

Fluent in Italian, she is dusky and thin,

My tutor from Ajmer has a major in Indian history,

'What's this?' I ask looking at her left wrist,

'This!' replies Ma'am Xona Berry, 'Is a sign of infinity.'

In the notebook, not electronic but rule,

I write words and figures as she recites,

"uno (1), due (2), tre (3), quattro (4),

il mio gatto piace il gelato",

My cat likes ice cream

Inspiring me to learn more.

Learning Italian is fun,

Sadly, the fear of drowning makes me run.

As in my third swim class, every two seconds I dip my head in and out,

Before I start to pout.

A nanny walks me to the bench and suggests I relax,

Out of the pool jumps my swim coach,

The six-feet muscular, coach Barbados.

Teal droplets trickling down his black skin,

Make the young and old ladies impazzire.

go crazy

Patting my back he sends me home,

I feel like a loser in low zone.

A sad pool incident I have to overcome,

A choice is given to me to continue or to run,

But I am not giving up,

Because I am supported by my teachers, dad and mum.

Coach Barbados isn't giving up on me either,

He gives me no pressure, but a breather.

Promising me to work on this together,

He demonstrates two experiments to perform,

At a nearby pond and in the Jacuzzi with water lukewarm.

A weekly visit to the pond is now a part of my routine,

Tri-weekly I must dip in the pool for ten seconds at an interval of five,

For the agenda is to be friends with water and with time dive.

How many relatives do you prank on and how many do you prank with?

It is the 3rd of July and she has arrived,

Chubby and fair with curly dark hair,

Aunt Veera Hue,

This time for a month, 'Oh Boy!' I mouthed,

Planning to seek refuge elsewhere by performing a stunt.

Bouncing on the couch she settles,

Distracting me are the peach triangles on the border of her blue saree,

My brown pupils enlarge,

An urge to learn appears in me maybe.

'Next Saturday will be your first thirty minutes class on knitting,' she says,

Joyful to see my sudden interest in linen.

On Wednesday evenings for an hour,

To the park mum, aunt and I go.

We see black fishes accompanying the brown ducks,

The caramel-skinned mongoose enjoying a few dips,

A mocha-coloured squirrel sprinting up and down the trunk,

The lush greenery and flowers white and pink,

The words I journal, fountain-like flow,

'Oh Boy!' I yell, celebrating my new mojo.

It's Friday and the next pupil will narrate their favourite tale or describe their hobby,

It's my turn and I talk about my progress on mastering the backstroke soon.

Swimming bi-weekly with coach Barbados, and weekly with dad,

Ma'am Xona and I resume our creative project of people surfing in water and rolling in sand.

A few rounds of Hangman my aunt Veera and I play,

Learning knitting, sharing our list of favourite things,

And reciting our created tongue twister,

"In Vegas wild Walt and wobbly Vani whine, until Vani waltzes wildly, and with a wasp, Walt wines."

We make memorable days.

On wrapped gifts for her husband and kids,

Painted elephant-shaped gift tags she tapes,

'Arrivederci!' said my cool aunt-friend, **goodbye**

After we plan to vacation next spring.

December is almost here,

The "Yay and Yum!" quarterly playdate is getting near,

Glass painting tiny plates and making cotton candy,

Moms are so cool,

What about you Dads? Why don't you try getting handy?

Half-giggly, half-grumpy, my classmate and soon-to-be-neighbour walks towards me,

Cane Foo with me, to school and back home daily,

A riddle for him one-way and artificial rest on the other,

Both ways keeping me no bother. ☺

I am in a lot of tension,

Because this week I am to be a part of an intervention.

Knitting is my new hobby and I am ecstatic,

But the colourful yarns are over,

Stopping me from completing the clover.

Adding to the list is my stationery,

Borrowing a few crayons and a pencil, I have my box filled.

'Yarns, notebooks, pencil, rubber, ruler, sharpener, crayons, paints, glue, scissors, sketch pens, chart paper, scrap book, and...' I recite,

Writing in black on my first whiteboard,

Ticking rubber, chart paper, paints and glue,

Foo! These aren't over too,

'A new slide!' I shriek,

My dainty bestie Fay Ona and I go closer and see a boy bent over,

Looking at each other we laugh,

Before running to the white, maroon-striped seesaw feeling daft.

Snacking at midnight, we knit a scarf for Uly her doll,

Glancing through my Italian notes,

She writes her first page of funny quotes.

A mock-up of a hot air balloon above a modelled skyscraper in fake grass,

On a round gold-rimmed wooden table with clear glass,

Earns us a standing ovation by the mass.

We applaud our teachers and janitors with claps and Thank You cards,

Because no matter the outcome of the competition,

We honour our school's decades long tradition.

Six weeks to day one of Class 3,

Ma'am Jinky has in her mind, this year's plan for my batchmates and me.

No picnic, no movies for the kids,

It is a four days trip.

Forty-nine of us to Vizag,

With teachers, Ma'am Jinky, Ma'am Niki and Ma'am Bay, and parents, aunties Giva, Dia and Zeh.

Playing dumb charades and baseball,

Building sand castles and jumping through waves,

Feeling down on quickly completing four days,

We return home with mini spade-shaped souvenirs and tanned faces.

The Swimming Association

On hearing the whistle blow, the competitors dive in and flow.

While we swiftly flap, the spectators hoot and clap.

Cheering for me are mum, dad, aunt Veera and Fay,

I am snapped for Ma'am Xona, Ma'am Jinky, cousin Omi and Cane.

Fifteenth in the first race and eleventh in the other,

Thrilled, coach Barbados gifts me a crab-themed cap.

Goggles in various shades, a pair per participant,

The Swimming Association too celebrates!

At home in lacrime-di-gioia we all rejoice,

happy tears

In zest I swallow a tablespoon of cocoa powder, realizing it wasn't wise.

Surrounded by golden streamers on lime green walls,

I cut the rectangular brown cake on the table covered with a white lace cloth.

Pouches and tiffin boxes I receive as gifts,

Candies, jellies and whistles fall from the dolphin piñata I tear-open,

Gorging on cake, chips and cheese balls,

Gulping down orange juice,

I plan to celebrate next year at an ocean.

www.ingramcontent.com/pod-product-compliance
Lightning Source LLC
LaVergne TN
LVHW061606070526
838199LV00077B/7189